The Hidden Colony

By McKenzie Walsh

Table Of Contents

The Oasis	4
Missions and Such	11
Falling Into Darkness	17
Creepy Crawlers	23
The Night Approaches	30
Coasting Home	37
Unexpected Visitors	45
Defending the Oasis	50
Escaping Destiny	57
Hope Is Restored	63
Safe At Last	68

The Oasis

    I scurried across the tiled floor as fast as my little legs could carry me trying to escape my impending doom. Now, some of you might ask what the heck is going on, we'll get to that, but first, let me tell you a little bit about myself. My name is Peter, and I'm the oldest of my family of 6. I have 3 brothers who are all absolute airheads. Then there's my sweet sister Lily; my mother absolutely adores her. Our Father died when we were very young, so it's just been us 6 for as long as I can remember.

    Now, this might seem like a semi-normal family, but we have one big difference. We're mice, but not just ordinary mice. We don't dig for scraps in garbage cans or live under cardboard boxes, we're civilized. We live in a community of mice ages young and old in an abandoned house that we call the Oasis. It's just off Main Street in the state of Maine. Ironic right? From the time our current mayor Mr. Figbottom discovered the abandoned house 3 years ago, our population has expanded greatly. Maine has become a very dangerous place for mice in the last decade, so all the misfits lucky enough to have stumbled upon this house have been greeted with open arms.

    Inside, our houses are dug into the sides of the walls. Most of us don't have much but we make do with what we have. For instance, my bed is made out of old cotton stuffing found inside a ripped-open teddy bear. Our bowls and cups are old cap bottles that we've found alongside the street. Even though it's not the fanciest, I love our tiny, cozy home.

    Now to some people, this might seem like a pretty good setup for a bunch of mice, but we have loads of problems. The winters are extremely hard times because there is simply not enough food for everyone. Last year I only ate a total of 5 peas and 2 lumps of bread for two months. I got so skinny my ribs were showing. We also have to worry about predators coming into the house, especially the town pest. The town pest is an old streaky brown cat by the name of Matilda who lives with the Johnsons across the street. She likes to visit every now and then to prey upon an unsuspecting mouse or two. But the biggest fear of all is the big men in blue jumpsuits.

    I personally have never seen these men in my short lifetime that I've lived in the safety of the Oasis, but let me tell you I've heard the most terrifying stories. They are called EXTERMINATORS... My neighbor Gertrude, who has lived long enough to see them, says that they have tortuous devices of all kinds. She says her family had been living in the attic of a small city apartment when these men showed up. They snatched up her mother and father in cold steel boxes and whisked them away. She never saw them again. Ever since then, she's lived in fear of them returning. Lots of my neighbors have similar stories to tell - geez- those kinds of stories give me nightmares.

To be safe from these people, we've built tunnels in the drywall that connect the entire Oasis. These tunnels connect to every house within. In the tunnels is where we also have our town hall, city square, and just about everything we need. In the giant halls of the Oasis, there is no evidence that we are even here. But on the inside, it is a bustling community of rodents. We've done this to ensure that no one could ever know we are all here and come after us (especially exterminators). I've never understood it, but for some reason, humans seem to think we're some type of plaque.

Now, to help ensure our survival, once you reach the age of 14 (that's about 4 months for all you human folks out there) we begin working. We all do our part to help our town and split all provisions equally. My mom is a teacher for young mice starting at the age of 3. Now you might be asking yourself what might you teach mice? It's not like we need to know Shakespeare or what elements are in the periodic table. No, what we learn is the history of our species, life outside the Oasis, and what things we can do for our survival.

    I personally believe I have the best job of all. I am what you call a seeker. I work for the only agency this town has. It's called Samy Soon's, and we are the backbone of this town. We get direct orders from the Mayor himself. We have a very versatile array of work that we do. Sometimes we go on expeditions to retrieve endangered mice in the surrounding areas, or even harvest food from the neighbor's garden across the alley. We do anything needed to help protect and ensure the safety of our town.

    I am actually scheduled for a mission today, but first I like to take my illegal morning jaunt around the house. This is illegal because technically unless you have special permission, mice are not permitted to walk the halls of the Oasis (mayor's orders), but I need my alone time. I can't stay cooped up in those stuffy tunnels all day. But what would absolutely give my mother a heart attack is that some days when I get bored of seeing those ugly bare walls of the Oasis, I sneak out the hole in one of the baseboards and go outside.

Outside is absolutely forbidden. Unless you're on a mission, mice under no circumstances are allowed to go outside. This is because a trip outside normally ends in you not coming back alive, but I love the thrill of being outside. Being on my own and sneaking along the tall grass surrounding the house is the thrill that I live for.

Anyways back to today. I was taking my regular walk in the morning when I rounded a corner, and there she was looming over me with those hungry eyes…Matilda. Uh Oh, I thought and did the only reasonable thing a mouse would do, I ran! I slid underneath an old rusty cabinet too small for Matilda to fit under. As she was swiping her paws at me, I poured a little bit of Catnip on her paw. When she withdrew it for another attempt it seemed as though it had done the trick because she stopped and sniffed it.

That distracted her just long enough to give me an opening to make a break for it. I took off once again, but as I looked back I saw maybe the Kat Nip wasn't such a good idea. Matilda was bouncing off the walls with energy, unfortunately, all that energy was focused on me. She took off in my direction, and although I had a head start she was gaining on me quickly. I knew if I didn't do something quickly, I was gonna end up as her morning snack. All I had to do was make it to the other hall around the corner and I could get into the tunnels through one of the entrance doors. But by then Matilda would have already gotten me.

Then my saving grace came. Max, my best friend, appeared out of nowhere with a water gun. Everybody knows how much cats hate water, so I thanked my lucky stars when I saw that. Max aimed the gun straight at Matilda's approaching face and fired. Bullseye! The water landed straight on Matilda's nose. Just as quickly as she had appeared, she left, making a beeline for the exit. Max and I ran straight to the entrance doors and breathing heavily slammed them shut.

Missions and Such

    I guess I should tell you a little bit about Max. He's been my best friend ever since we were little. Our friendship started when he threw a tomato at the class bully in 2nd grade. He's the second closest thing to family. He's more like a brother to me than my real brothers. We spend just about every second of the day together doing just about anything we want. And the best part is that we work together at Samy Soon's. Every mission I go on, he's there with me. I know he's always got my back and I've got his.

Anyways, as soon as we closed the door I slowly looked over to see Max glaring at me. "I know what you're gonna-" I couldn't finish because Max interrupted me.

"Don't even try to make excuses. You know I don't approve of you leaving the safety of the walls unaccompanied. I tell you this all the time and you don't listen to me. Now thank God I had a gut feeling something was wrong or else who knows what would have happened to you. Now please promise me for real this time that you're not going to do that again."

"Ok, I won't," I said because I knew that was the only way he would ever let this go. But I have a feeling that won't be the last time I do that.

"Ok good," Max said. "Now let's get a move on, we're already late for work, thanks to your little stunt."

As Max and I headed down the long, crowded hallway tunnel we were stopped multiple times by friends of my mom's. They were mainly telling me to say hello from them. Apparently, everyone here loves my mom, even though I have a feeling they wouldn't feel the same way if they lived with her. Once we had bypassed most of the traffic, we were almost to the end of the hall where we could see the old, rickety sign reading Samy Soon's. As soon as we pushed open the door, standing there was our boss, Ms. Cricket.

Ms. Cricket is about as nasty as bosses come. She always has a target on Max and I, and gives us the least desirable missions out of every agent here. Everyone says it's because we're the youngest, but I know it's because she's jealous of our friendship. She's scared away every possible friend that she's ever had.

"Well good morning, if it isn't the dynamic duo themselves coming in late. I expect this from Peter, but you Max, wow, definitely expected better from you." Ms. Cricket said.

"Oh give us a break will ya," I said exhausted. "Anyways, what's our mission for today?"

"Well I have a treat for you two," She said. "One of our spotters found a mouse family of 5 living in the gutters of 2234 Wilson Street. That's two blocks away from here. They overheard the people living there saying that they were going to have an exterminator come and remove them. This family has no idea this is happening. Your mission is to retrieve them and bring them back here within two days, or it will be too late."

" Ok, we'll gear up quickly and leave as soon as possible," Max said.

The two of us headed to the back room to grab what we needed. For missions, all the supplies in the back room are "free for all." The first thing I grabbed was my standard black backpack made out of recycled leather. I had once found the leather in a garbage bin near the house. Next, I grabbed: a sack of poppy seeds, some rope made out of braided whiskers, my knife from an old pop can, some clean water in a "flask", and a map of the surrounding neighbors hood. On the map, I located 2234 Wilson Street. Using prior knowledge I constructed the most desirable route.

I assumed Max grabbed the same stuff, but I just hope whatever he grabbed will be useful to us, because I don't have time to double-check. I saw my friend Trina, who is also a Seeker walk by. I told her to let my mom know I'll be out on a mission.

"Will do, and Peter," Trina said, "be careful, I know you're trained for this but two blocks is a long way."

"Thanks Trina I will. Max and I will be back in no time!" Although I barely believed myself. The truth is I've never traveled that far from the Oasis before, but what could go wrong? Well, a lot of things. But for my sanity, I'm not even going to think about it.

The two of us wandered over to the exit door. We did our ritual handshake and were about to leave when we were stopped. Of course, it was Ms. Cricket, what did she want?

"You boys didn't think it was just the two of you on this mission did you?"

"Ya sorta, we've never done it any differently," Max said.

"Well think again, Jasmine will be accompanying you two on this mission." She stared directly into my soul, "And if I hear that your guys fighting compromised the mission in any way, you'll all be demoted to desk duty for the next month."

"Oh no," Max said, "anyone but her she's the devil himself."

"Nope, I don't want to hear it. All three of you will do this mission together and that's that."

Oh lord, I hate Jasmine (or as my mom would say extremely disliked) . Ever since we were kids she's tormented Max and I. I remember one year she put burrs on my seat and I didn't realize until I already sat down. They stuck to my fur like glue and my mom had to cut them out the best she could. For weeks I got made fun of because I had a patch of hair missing on my butt... on my butt!

Oh course I could tell Jasmine wasn't a fan of this news either, but she was such a suck-up she would never say anything. I wanted to let her know who was in charge here, so I went up to her and said, "If you just do what Max and I tell you to and everything will be fine."

But of course, she had to be her difficult self, because she said, "Ummm no, you two stay out of my way and we won't have another incident like when your butt was as bare as my countertop." And with that, she stormed off towards the door.

Max whispered under his breath, "Welp this is going to suck." Boy, I couldn't agree more, and we followed her out the door.

Falling Into Darkness

   The door is just a crack in the house that leads right into the bottom of the gutter pipe. This pipe runs right along the side of the house. "Whoo," I yelled as I slid down the rest of the pipe and shot out onto the overgrown lawn. I stumbled onto the ground, and once I got my footing I looked over to see Max also struggling to get up. But of course, Jasmine was already up and moving.
   "Hey, wait up," I yelled. As we chased after her.
   "Shhhhh, do you guys ever shut up? God I can't believe I got paired up with you idiots, I mean you can't be trusted to tie a knot, and yet you get

assigned a 2 block mission. I don't know what Ms. Cricket was thinking with this one."

"Oh god, here we go again. Hi I'm Jasmine, and I'm so much better than everyone else," Max said annoyed. "Look, we're not happy to be here doing this with you either, but let's all just try to get along for the mission's sake."

"Fine," Jasmine said, "but I'm not going to be picking up after your mistakes."

"Wasn't planning on it," Max said.

The three of us crawled through the overgrown grass so as to not be spotted by the hawks flying overhead. Just as we were about to make it to the edge of the sidewalk, I saw a huge shadow, so I looked up. Playing out in the street were three braced-faced little girls riding around on their tricycles. One had the biggest lollipop I'd ever seen in her hand. Another had the head of a teddy bear stuck onto the front of her bike, and the last one had a gigantic snot rocket hanging from her nose.

"Hide," I squeaked, but it was too late. The girl with the lollipop had already seen us.

She yelled to her friends, "Hey look over there, there's some mice. Let's catch them and then we can play doctor with them." The three girls started riding over in our direction.

"Run," Max screamed. We all made a mad dash for the house, but the girls were much faster than us. One of them circled in front of us and cut off our only escape route. Then they started attacking. All three of them rode straight at us. They were going to run us over! I had just narrowly jumped out of the way to avoid one of them when I looked over at Max. He was looking the wrong way and the snot-nosed girl was going straight at him.

"Max lookout," I yelled. He jumped out of the way just at the last second I thought. But then I saw him start limping off, so I knew he was hurt. Jasmine ran over to me and screamed panicking, "What are we going to do? We're trapped!"

"No, look over there," I yelled pointing to a storm gutter just on the edge of the street. " We can't go back inside the Oasis or we might lead them straight to everybody. If we can just get over there, we can climb inside and wait them out." Just as I said that a shuddering tremble of the ground sent both of us on our butts. The girls were throwing rocks at us now, and not tiny pebbles, but the kind of rocks that break windows. "You go get Max and get in the drain, I'll distract them," I yelled.

"Ok," Jasmine said, and she took off towards Max.

The girls were pretty spread out, so I figured my best bet was to target one individually and divert all of their attention to me. As I got closer to the girl with the lollipop, she started chucking rocks at me. I narrowly dodged the first two, and by then I was close enough that she started to ride her bike at me.

Luckily she wasn't very coordinated at riding her bike. So as she came by me I ran right between the training wheels and pulled myself up onto the peddle. I held on for dear life. The girl had no idea I was there, so I took advantage of this. Slowly I moved up to where her foot was and grabbed her shoelace. I pulled back the top of her sock, opened my mouth as wide as I could, and bit down.

Then the loudest shriek I've ever heard came right out of her mouth. The bike toppled over with both her and me on it. When I hit the ground it was the worst pain ever. My whole body shook, but I knew I had to get up. I couldn't stay there. I got up and started running.

Just up ahead of me, I could see Jasmine helping carry Max into the drain. I thought everything was good until I looked back. I was right about one thing, I had diverted the girls' attention away from my friends, but not myself. One of the girls was over helping her hurt friend, but the other one was coming straight for me.

Apparently, all I had done was manage to make her angry. She was riding so fast towards me that her snot was getting pushed back in the wind. Max and Jasmine were already in the drain yelling at me to hurry. Ya, duh guys, that's my plan. I was only 10 feet away from the drain when the girl tauntingly started yelling, "I'm gonna get you, I'm gonna get you."

Right as I could feel the tires almost hitting my heel, I jumped. I landed right in Max's arms. I was going so fast though, that when I went into him I couldn't stop. My momentum took Max, Jasmine, and I right off the ledge and we all fell into the deep depths of the sewer. As I was falling into the darkness, all I could see was a small box of light slowly fading away.

Creepy Crawlers

Plop, we all landed in brown, foul-looking water. Jasmine, who keeps her hair smelling fresh all the time, let out a horrible scream. "Aghhghghh, oh my gosh disgusting! Great going, Peter. Now I smell like Guss that old rat from the East Side."

"Shut up," I said. "I didn't mean to push us all down here. Now let's just find a way to get out. Look, there's a ledge, let's swim over to it."

"Hellpppp," Max screamed. "I can't swim!"

I swam over to Max and pulled him along the water to the ledge. Jasmine was already on the ledge when we got over there, so she helped me hoist Max up. Then I pulled myself up and assessed the damage. My backpack was made out of leather, so everything inside including the map was dry, thank goodness.

Then I looked over at Max who was clutching his leg. "What happened?" I asked.

"When that girl rode her bike at me, I tried to jump out of the way, but she caught my hind leg. I can't put any pressure on it, I think it's broken."

"Oh god, ok, let's put a stint on it." I grabbed my knife from my backpack and tied it upright on Max's leg with some rope. "Let's hope that helps for now. Let's find a way out of here," I said.

"And how do you plan on doing that Sherlock?" Jasmine asked. The sewer runs for miles everywhere we look, and any ladders out are too high up for us to reach.

"I don't know," I said truthfully, "but if we don't try, the last thing you'll ever see are these green, slimy walls. If I look at the map, we're basically underneath the Oasis right now. It shows we're not too far away from being underneath the Shadows Stream. Maybe if we're lucky the sewer will connect to the stream and we can get out."

"Ok," Max said, "That sounds like our best option, let's do it." But as he started to stand up his face went white and I had to catch him before he fell.

"Are you going to be alright walking that far?" I asked.

"Truthfully I don't know, but I have to try."

"Ok, good. Since Jasmine always boasts about how strong she is, I'm sure she would be more than happy to aid you in walking there." I looked over to Jasmine with a sly smile.

"Ughhh fine, if I have to do everything around here. Let's go." Jasmine walked over to Max and while they were getting situated, I took another look at the map.

"So it looks like if we keep going straight for a bit and then take a left we should be there within the next hour or two," I said. I looked over at Max and caught a gaze with him and winked. At least by this happening, we finally were able to put Jasmine in her place.

Just like that, we were off. To help pass the time Max and I sang Ghost Mices' new album *Rockers*, and we even got Jasmine to join in a little bit. But, it wasn't long until trouble started to happen. The farther along we got into the sewer the worst and worst smell we encountered. Of course, we didn't think much of it, because, after all, sewers are supposed to smell. It wasn't until we had taken that left to take us the rest of the way to the hopeful exit, that everything went downhill.

All of a sudden, the three of us were yanked from the ground all the way to the first rung of a ladder. I was hanging upside down staring at the ground, when four of the biggest rats I'd ever seen came into view. They were saying something I didn't understand, but apparently, Jasmine did, because she started howling as loud as she could.

"No no no, let us down. We didn't mean to come down here, just let us go!" That definitely didn't work. Instead of letting us go, they did the opposite. They lowered us to the ground and bound up our hands and feet. Then they connected us to a stick and started carrying us. Except for Max. When they tried to bind up his feet he started yelping so badly because of his leg, that the biggest rat had to carry him over his back.

They took turn after turn until finally, they led us into a big room. All along the walls was big red graffiti which I had no idea what it meant. At the end of the room sat an old gray rat on a chair made of chopsticks. They dropped us in the middle of the whole room and untied us.

"What's going on-" Max started to say, but one of the rats stuck a big smelly finger on his lips.

"Shhhhhh," was all the rat said, but it definitely was enough to quiet us up.

"Who are these rats?" I whispered over to Jasmine.

"They're called the Crawlers. They've lived down in the sewers for decades. No one knows much about them except for the story that once a group of people went down in the sewers once for maintenance. They had run into the Crawlers, and were never heard from again."

"And you didn't think this would be worth mentioning earlier," I asked slightly appalled.

"No well I'd heard about them before, but I thought it was just a myth. Apparently, it wasn't."

"Ya, it sure wasn't," I said.

"Silence," the old gray rat said, commanding our attention. "Now what have we caught in our traps? Three young and shining mice? Where are you all from?"

"The Oasis," I said quickly, "it's an abandoned house not far from here."

"Oh, I know what the Oasis is. For as long as I can remember residents in the Oasis have been snarky uptight mice, who think they're so much better than us sewer rats. Well, I'll show them. What are you all doing down here?" he asked.

"It's a long story. We got chased by these little girls and the only way to escape was by going into the storm drain," said Jasmine.

" Well isn't that a shame for you, looks like I'll be getting some new rugs. Jermaine, please escort these mice to the boiler room, and make quick work of them."

"No please, we've got to get back to the surface, please help us," Jasmine whined annoyingly as we were getting carried off. "Now why would I help you? You know, my half-brother founded the Oasis. And yet when I asked him if my crew could live up there, he laughed in my face. This will be a taste of your own medicine."

"Wait!" Jasmine screamed, "Just listen to me please."

"Fine, I'll entertain you, little girl. You have thirty seconds, don't waste my time."

"Ok, look. Yes, it sounds like you have unsolved problems with your brother, but we aren't a part of that. The three of us are Seekers and were actually on a mission right now. We need to get to a house and evacuate a family of mice before an exterminator arrives."

"Hmmm," the rat thought. "As much as I hate everyone and anyone from the Oasis, I hate exterminators even more. I'll let you go just this once, but if I ever see you down here again, that'll be your end. Jermaine shows them the way out."

"Thank you so much," I exclaimed. Jermaine led us all down a dimly lit hallway until we finally reached a door.

Jermaine opened the door and said, "Your lucky, boss doesn't normally make exceptions like this. Now once you go through that door there will be a ramp that takes you up to a park. Now go quickly before he changes his mind."

The Night Approaches

It took us what felt like ages to get up that steep ramp. When we finally reached the top and shoved open the door, there was grass. Freshly cut grass, and leaves. Oh, beautiful leaves of all colors. I sprung out onto the grass and rolled over so many times I lost count. "Land, land, of beautiful land, I'll never leave you again," I exclaimed.

Jasmine and Max were looking at me like I'd lost my mind. I didn't care though, we almost died in that sewer. I'll never take land above the sewer for granted again.

"Alright that's enough Peter," Jasmine said, "we get it, we're lucky to be alive, but we still have our mission to complete."

The sun was almost down by now. I thought to myself that it probably would do us no good to keep going for tonight. When it's dark, loads more creatures looking for an adorable bite-sized snack like us are out and about. I was about to say something along those lines when Max said it first.

"How about we sleep for tonight? My leg hurts awfully bad, and I think I might pass out if we travel anymore. I'm sure you two are exhausted as well. And plus we're less than a block away from that house. We'll have plenty of time to get to them tomorrow. Look at all that playground equipment just over there, we could find a little niche for us all to sleep in over there and call it a night."

"That's a good idea, Max. If we keep going while we're tired, who knows what could happen." I said and looked over to Jasmine hopefully. I thought she would put up more of a fight, but instead, she agreed.

" I think you guys are right, a good night's sleep is exactly what we need," she said.

The three of us headed over to the playground. We found a tight little opening in one of the sew-saws and climbed in. It wasn't the comfiest sleep I'd ever had. We were all pushed so close together that if someone moved just the slightest, it would throw everybody off. But apparently, that didn't stop all of us from sleeping way past how long we should have.

It wasn't until about mid-day that one of the kids trying to use the see-saw woke us up. I had started feeling a pinching sensation when I awoke to realize we were getting squashed from the see-saw being in use. "Wake uppppp!" I screamed. "We need to get out of here," I yelled while shoving Max and Jasmine awake.

"What's going on?" Max asked in a raspy voice.

"What's going on is that we need to get out here ASAP!" I screamed as I pulled all three of us out of the niche. We landed softly on the styrofoam ground, but it was just enough to wake Jasmine up. She seemed to realize what was going on and took off running towards some bushes at the end of the park. Max and I slowly hobbled over there. I was absolutely winded by the time we made it to the bushes and climbed inside.

"What time is it?" Jasmine shrieked.

"I don't know," I said, "but we definitely slept too long. We need to leave right now if we want a chance at making it to that family in time."

"Agreed," Max said.

I looked at the map and concluded that the quickest route to the house would be to cut across the busy road next to the park. From there we could make a straight bee-line through the alley and get to the house. I told Max and Jasmine my plan, and they both agreed that was the best route to take. The hard part was going to be crossing that street though. With four lanes of non-stop traffic this would be difficult.

We went over to the edge of the sidewalk where no people were occupying it. "I think our best bet is to run straight across the street and hope for the best," I said.

"Some people might try to avoid us, but I doubt it," Jasmine said.

"Ok, let's go. We're running out of time. 1, 2, 3 go!" Max yelled. I was helping Max walk, so I was most worried for us. We wouldn't be able to make as quick of maneuvers as Jasmine. She was way ahead of us already, making it to the middle with ease.

"Let's try to wait for an opening," Max said.

"Ok, look here after this blue car we should be able to get to the middle at least," I said.

As soon as the blue car passed by, we took off as fast as we could. We were almost in the middle when a motorcycle came out of nowhere. We lunged as far as we could to avoid the oncoming motorcycle. We did manage to not get run over, but we ended up being scraped up pretty badly from that rough road. I looked up to see Jasmine had already made it across and was cheering for us to make it.

We got back up on our paws and ran trying to make it through one of the gaps. We didn't time it well enough though, because one of the cars was coming straight for us. As the big black tires got closer, my life flashed before my eyes. There was no way out of this, we were going to be flattened right here on this road. I started to think about my family and what they would do without me. But right then, I heard a screeching noise. The car had stopped.

I couldn't believe it. Why had they stopped? It didn't matter though, Max and I were both still alive. We stumbled the rest of the way off the street and lay down exhausted. We couldn't lie down for long though, we had to keep going.

By now Max was almost entirely useless. Jasmine and I both had to help carry him. This really slowed us down. We made it to the alley right after that. We walked along the edge so as not to be seen, and made it all the way to the house unscathed. We shimmied through a crack in the fencing and went into the backyard.

The backyard was beautiful. It had a water fountain and a gigantic vegetable garden. No wonder the family lived here. This is a beautiful place to raise baby mice. Anyways, time to evacuate this family. We left Max just at the bottom edge of the house, and Jasmine and I climbed up the vines to the roof. But when we got to the roof we could tell something was off.

It was like the world got darker. At first, we couldn't see the family, but we figured they were just hidden in the gutters. The two of us searched for quite some time until I looked over the edge of the roof and saw something very troubling. In the street was a car that had "We'll get rid of all your nasty pests- Landfill Exterminators" written in big blue letters on the side. Standing off to the side of the car was a big man holding cages. But when I looked closely I saw the mice we had been sent to evacuate in them.

    Jasmine and I looked at each other. We didn't know what to do. Could we try to overtake the man, and get them free? But it was already too late because when we looked over there again, the car was driving off.

    I got a numb feeling throughout my entire body. I'd never failed a mission before. Who knows what the exterminator would do with the mice, I didn't even want to think about it. If only we hadn't thought of ourselves and gone to sleep, the family would still be safe. Jasmine and I slumped over to the edge of the roof and slid down the vines. Max was waiting there asking us what happened, but I just walked right past. In fact, I kept on walking all the way back to the Oasis.

Coasting Home

      By the time the sun was setting, I had made it back to the Oasis. I slipped through the tiny crack near the big green bushes and entered back into the main part of Samy Soons. The first thing I saw was Trina working over by the supply closet, and I fell to the ground. She ran over to me asking what was wrong, but I couldn't even get a word out. All I could do was cry. I cried for what felt like forever until I was so exhausted that I simply passed out.

      I wouldn't wake up again till a whole day later. I slept through the whole night and part of the next day. When I woke up I was back in my cozy room with tons of food laying on my bedside table. There was a slice of bread, a jar of seeds, a slice of cheese, and some water in a cleaned-out glue stick cap. I shakingly moved my hand over to the table and slowly picked up the water forcing myself to drink at least a few sips.

"Knock knock," I heard someone say as they slowly opened the door. It was my mother. For some reason seeing her at this moment was very comforting after the last couple of days I have had. "Hi honey, how are you doing?" She asked gently, as she came over and sat on the edge of my bed. "I heard what happened on your mission, I'm very sorry it didn't go the way you would have liked."

"That's one way to sum it up, I just feel like I failed that family. We could have easily made it there on time. Who knows what is happening to them? Now that they're with those exterminators, they might not even be alive right now." I said I was so disappointed in myself. " Max and Jasmine made it back alright, right? I know I kinda just left them behind, but I figured they'd be alright."

"Yes, they're fine. They got back not long after you did. It sounds like Max went straight to the infirmary to get his leg taken care of. And of course, Jasmine is as good as new. You could probably go see him today if you're feeling up to it."

Right then there was a knock on the back door connected to the tunnels. My mom got up to go see who it was, and I sat back in my bed trying to hear the conversation. It was a familiar voice, but I couldn't quite place my finger on who it was. It sounded like the mouse was coming into our house, and the footsteps were getting closer. Then Jasmine popped her head around the corner of my door and came in.

"Oh hi, I'm sorry I wasn't expecting to see you, or I would have made myself a bit more presentable," I said as I sat up in my bed. "What's up?"

"Well, first of all, I need you to apologize for leaving Max and me back there on the mission. No matter what happens we don't leave each other. I had to carry him back all by myself, and what if we had run into a stray cat, that would have been a huge problem. Who knows if we would have made it back." Jasmine said.

"I know, I'm sorry. I shouldn't have done that. I wasn't thinking, I just wanted to get out of there." I said.

"It's ok I understand how you felt, just make sure it doesn't happen again."

"Again? I don't think there will be any again after that. There's no way Ms. Cricket hasn't fired me by now." I said.

Jasmine replied," No way, Ms.Cricket might hate you with all her guts, but she knows how good of an agent you are. These kinds of things happen on rare occasions. Anyways, let me get to what I came here to say. All hope is not lost yet, last night Ms. Cricket sent out a sting operation compiled of some of our best agents. They're going to the exterminator's office, and hopefully, they might find the family somewhere there. Odds are they'll still be there, and we might be able to bring them all here without a single scratch."

That's good, I thought. Maybe we could fix this mistake after all.

"Earlier today, Ms.Cricket told me to bring you to her as soon as you wake up. So get ready and we're gonna head out. But first, we're gonna go see Max and check on how he's doing," Jasmine said.

"Ok," I said and got out of bed. I grabbed the slice of bread next to my bed and slapped the cheese on top. To finish it off I sprinkled some seeds on it. I also grabbed my backpack, threw it on my back, and was ready to go. We stopped in my kitchen to say bye to my mom. I told her Ms. Cricket wanted to talk to me and I would hopefully be back soon.

"Alright, I love you, come back in one piece please!" She said as Jasmine and I headed out the door.

I was back in the tunnels. It was refreshing to be back in the safety of the Oasis after my run-in with sewer rats and killer kids. We walked over to the infirmary, which was pretty close to my house, and walked through the door. I'd never actually been inside of here before except for when I was very young. I needed some stitches after cutting myself on the edge of my bed, but I didn't remember what this place looked like at all.

However, it does look like we have focused a lot of time on making this place as up-to-date as possible. There were tons of rooms with foam chunks (these are very nice beds in the Oasis). There was also a fully stocked supply closet filled with: needles, yarn, makeshift bandages, and even some medicine that we had once stolen from a veterinary office.

    Jasmine said Max was in room six, so we made our way back there. When we went into the room, the only doctor in the Oasis was speaking with Max. He had a little piece of paper and was taking notes. Max looked a little worse for wear, but he was still smiling. When he saw us come into the room his face lit up.

    The doctor saw us come in too, and he said, "Well if it isn't the other two musketeers. Max is going to be fine, he's just not going to be able to put any weight on his hind leg for a few weeks. Now I'll leave so you all can talk, but make it quick he needs his rest."

    "Ok will do, thanks doc," I said as I migrated over to his bed. The doctor left the room and finally, the three of us could really talk. "I'm so sorry Max, this is all my fault. And to make things worse, I left you two back there to fend on your own. I'm a terrible friend."

"Now you listen here," he said, " You're not a bad friend. You were upset, and I understand. But you also need to realize something, we were all in it together, and it's all our fault. You're not the only mouse who needs to take responsibility for that family, ok?"

"Ya, ok," I said. "And hey look, Jasmine told me some other agents already headed out to retrieve the family. Hopefully, if all goes well they'll be here soon. Anyways, we just wanted to see how you were doing before we head over to Samy Soon's. Apparently, Ms. Cricket wants to talk to me, and I know it can't be anything good."

"I already knew all that. You've been asleep for a long time ya know. Keep up." Max said.

"Ok whatever, at least I can walk," I said jokingly, "We'll be back a bit later to check on you". From there Jasmine and I headed back out to the tunnels.

By the time Jasmine and I made it to Samy Soon's, I was exhausted. I guess I wasn't feeling like myself, but I forced on a smile and soldiered on. We reached the door and pushed it open to see everyone running about in a panic.

Unexpected Visitors

What's going on? I thought to myself. Everybody was moving a thousand miles an hour and the whole place was in total disarray. I saw Trina hustling over to her 'desk' and tried to stop her and ask what was going on, but all she could muster up was, "Ask Ms. Cricket," and she hustled off.

I looked at Jasmine to see if she knew, but she looked just as confused. We scurried over to where we knew Ms. Cricket would be. She was in her office bossing everyone around as usual. When Jasmine and I walked through the doorway, Ms.

Cricket saw us out of the corner of her eye and she stopped dead in her tracks.

"You two, come with me now!" She yelled and marched over to the meeting room with the two of us hot on her tail. When we got to the meeting room, I saw that there were a few other agents waiting there. She slammed the door shut and sat down in a heap of stress. With her head slumped in her hands she let out a groan and sighed. "Oh this is not good, not good at all," she said, shaking her head.

"What's not good," I asked, "What's going on, why is everyone running around like the world is ending?"

"Because it basically is," she snapped at me. "Now, let's get down to business, shall we? I've gathered you all here because you are some of the best agents that we have here at Samy Soon's. Not too long ago, I received a direct letter from the Mayor himself with the same information I'm about to tell all of you." She said shakingly.

"Earlier today we received word that the Oasis has been sold to a human family. Now we all thought this place was abandoned, but apparently, someone still owned it, and now they've sold it. The family will be coming any hour today. They'll have moving trucks and more manpower than we've ever seen. Once they realize there's a colony of mice living here, it's game over for us. Tons of exterminators will swamp these halls taking every last one of us. We need to evacuate ASAP. We've prepared for something like this. We set up provisions and enough room for everyone to at least fit into a hollowed-out Chestnut Tree in the forest not far from here. But of course, we never thought something like this would happen so close in the future. We are still far from being ready. We'll just have to make do with what we have. I've sent out Trina and Kyle to round up everyone into the town square as we speak. We're going to start evacuating as soon as possible."

    While she was saying this my mind was moving a mile per minute. I started thinking about my mom and Lily. Oh how they must be so scared right now, and what if they don't bring the right things with them? What if they forget food and water, or what if they forget to bring my dad's old watch? That was his favorite belonging, and I'd be heartbroken if we lost it. And even though my brothers were the definition of annoying, I still cared about them. I hoped they would be smart enough to get out with everyone else, and not try and stay behind. This was all pressing to me, but I needed to stay focused on what Ms. Cricket was saying.

"Now, you're all probably wondering why I've gathered you all up personally to tell you this. I've selected you 4 to be our distraction. This isn't to put you in harm's way but to make sure we have enough time to evacuate. This will be the most important job you ever do. If the people do show up before everyones' out, you need to stop them long enough for us all to escape. Do you understand?" She asked all of us who had blank expressions on our faces.

Jasmine shook her head, and we all followed her lead.

"Good," Ms. Cricket said. "Now go post yourselves near both the front and back entrances. Do whatever you have to do to stop them. Oh and Peter, Jasmine?" She asked almost compassionately.

"Yes?" I asked.

"Don't worry about Max, I'll personally make sure he gets out of here ok." She said and hustled off to deal with everyone else.

I took in the other pair of agents in the room. I'd seen them before on many occasions but never bothered to learn their names. Begrudgingly, I told them Jasmine and I could take the front entrance. This was because the people would obviously be coming in through those doors, and I wouldn't feel right sending those two head-on into trouble. The pair nodded relieved they weren't going to be taking the front entrance, and rushed off to get to the back entrance.

Once the two of them left, Jasmine and I made one last trip to the supply room. I already had my backpack with me, so I grabbed all I could. We decided we should set up some booby traps of sorts to distract the people before they could get to the porch. Once we were satisfied with our loot, we headed through the tunnels to the front entrance.

My house was on the way to the front. When we were about to pass it, I stopped to check in and say goodbye to everyone. The door was already cracked open, but when I went in, I couldn't find anyone. That was a good sign at least, everyone got out in time. The whole place was ransacked by my mom and Lily packing in a rush. Laying on the cabinet was my father's watch. It looked like they planned on taking it, but must have forgotten. No worries though, I slipped it on my wrist and closed the door taking in my childhood home for one last time. We went back out into the tunnels and trekked on to the front.

    We reached the front entrance in no time and slid through the crack in the door. The neighborhood looked the same as ever, but the air just felt colder. There on the overgrown front lawn stood the taunting sold sign for all to see. I still don't understand how this happened so fast. The one place I felt safe from people, will no longer be in just a few hours. I just hope we can hold these people off long enough so everyone can escape. If not, the whole colony could be at risk of being found.

Defending the Oasis

We had no time to spare. Jasmine and I crawled out to the front of the walkway as we tried to avoid being spotted, and got straight to work. For the first 'trap', we used a whole bucket of tiny clear beads. The two of us spread them out on the middle of the sidewalk that goes to the front porch of the house. The plan is to hopefully have someone slip on them, causing them to take more time getting to the house.

To set up the next 'trap' we used a thin line of whisker rope. Jasmine held one end and I held the other. We unraveled the rope and tied it as tight as we could to both the bush and the mailbox. This was not far down from where the bead trap was. We're hoping this will trip at least one of them.

That was all we had time to set up. As we were crawling back to the house, suddenly a group of pigeons landed right in our path. Uh oh, I thought, any animal that could fly and had a beak was dangerous. Jasmine seemed to be thinking the exact same thing because we both started running the opposite way of the pigeons.

Then, two of the pigeons took up flight and landed right in front of us, once again blocking our escape route. Jasmine and I stopped dead in our tracks and circled around looking for any way out. But right then, one of the pigeons snatched me up by the end of my tail. I could feel myself getting lifted off the ground, so I kicked and bit with all my might until I fell hard back to the ground.

Then the pigeons started to enclose us in a circle. I'd never had any issues with pigeons before, but I assumed I was about to. Thankfully, one of them, who I assumed was the leader, started yelling at all the pigeons.

"Stoppppp!! What are you idiots doing? I told you not to attack them. Geez it's like your brains are the size of an almond!" The small gray and white pigeon said, giving an angry look over at his friends.

"Hi, let us start over," he said as he hobbled to where Jasmine and I were. " My name is Henry. I'm in charge of the West Park pigeon flock. I saw you guys over in my park a couple of days ago, and I was very intrigued as to what all of you were doing there."

"Oh um we were just scavenging for food," I lied. What? I'm not about to spill the secrets of the Oasis to a bunch of random pigeons.

"I know you're lying. If you don't tell me the truth about what you were doing in my park, we're going to have a problem." He said, twisting his head into an awkward position. The other pigeons started to get closer and closer, slowly tightening the circle. To be honest, I wasn't quite sure what was going on. I don't understand the big deal that we were in his park. I also didn't understand why he needed to know what we were doing there. But we didn't have time to deal with this nonsense, so I tested my luck and told him the truth.

"Look," I said, "We don't want any trouble. We were just passing through your park trying to get a family of mice back safely to our colony. We didn't mean to sleep there, it just kind of happened. But trust me we weren't doing anything shady." I said hoping this pigeon (who seemed to be on a massive power trip) would just leave us alone.

For quite some time he stared right into my eyes. It actually made me quite uncomfortable. Then after what felt like ages, he exclaimed in a disturbingly loud voice, "Well I believe you! Just had to make sure you mice weren't doing anything weird in my park. You have to be careful, there are lots of nut jobs out there."

Ya right, I thought. There's a nut job standing right in front of me.

"Sorry about the inconvenience." He said. Then he pointed at the pigeon who had caught me by my tail." Jerry is still learning. Anyways, let me know if I can do anything to make this up to you my friends," he said joyously. He started to fly away when Jasmine called out.

"Actually there is," she said. "There are some people who will be coming any time now to move into the house right there. Our whole colony lives there, but we haven't evacuated everyone yet. We've set up two booby traps to slow them down, but if they make it past those we might need your help."

Henry the pigeon got an excited look on his face. "What do you want us to do?" He was intrigued. Jasmine pulled him aside and laid out her plan. Henry almost started jumping up and down when he heard it. He rounded up the rest of his flock, and they flew off to a nearby tree waiting to set the plan into motion.

I went up to Jasmine to ask what the plan was, but she told me to wait and see. The two of us headed back to the house for real this time. Once we got to the porch we hid behind some of the rods of the railing. This way we were hidden, but still able to see the street and the stream of mice still evacuating the house.

The first 10 minutes passed by very slowly. Jasmine and I had our backs to each other so we could watch each end of the street. At first, we stood there in silence, but then Jasmine started talking. "Look Peter, I know we've never really gotten along. But seeing as we're about to face some pretty dangerous stuff, I figure I should be honest with you. The truth is the reason I was so mean to you when we were kids was because I liked you. I was so mean to you because I didn't think you liked me back, which made me angry. And even on our last mission, I was mean to you, because I…still like you." She said uncomfortably.

Ummmm hold up, did I just hear that right? Jasmine, the girl who had tormented me my entire life, had a crush on me? No way, I didn't believe it… But then in the awkward silence that followed that confession, I started thinking, maybe I liked her too.

"Oh um thank you for telling me Jasmine," I said blushing (even though she couldn't see my face, I was still embarrassed). "That kind of makes sense of why you treated me like that as a kid. But you know you could have just told me that, it would have made things easier." I said

"I know," she said, "but I didn't know what else to do, so here we are. Do you like me at all?" she asked shyly.

"Honestly, when I think about it I think I do. I used to like you when we were little, but I brushed it aside because I always figured you hated me. Hey, if we make it out of here, we can go on a real date." I said. "We can walk down to the river or something, and watch the fireflies buzz around."

"Ya I would like that," Jasmine said. She was about to say something else when the screech of tires interrupted her. A red minivan covered in dirt had come to a stop right in front of the house. I guess I was so distracted by what Jasmine was saying, I hadn't even seen it pull up.

Escaping Destiny

From out of the car stepped the human family. First, came the daughter. She was probably no older than 5, and she was wearing a cute little yellow sundress with white shoes. Then out came the son. He must be about 10 years old. He was wearing brown glasses and had his head buried in a book. Then out stepped the mother from the driver's seat. She looked like a relatively nice lady, but she had extremely dark bags under her eyes and looked exhausted. She was currently preoccupied with trying to steer her daughter onto the sidewalk. Lastly, out came the father from the passenger side door. He seemed to be in a deep conversation with a lady wearing pearls and a pantsuit. She must be the realtor agent.

"Oh boy, you're just going to love this place! It's probably a little bit of a fixer-upper, but with a young family like yours I'm sure you can make it into your dream home." The realtor said as she started leading the family down the sidewalk to the front door.

"Yes, I remember seeing this house a couple of years ago, when the owner first moved out. Let's just hope it's still in good condition, seeing as I'm going to pay a fortune for it. Oh, and since it has been vacant for a few years, I'm also hoping no pesky rodents have found their way into the house. It'll be a hassle to try and hire an exterminator on such short notice." The father said in an exasperated voice.

Jasmine and I looked at each other with great concern. Quietly, I said, "Let's hope these traps work. Look, the little girl is almost to the beads." I said pointing over to where the girl was. I was holding my breath watching her get closer and closer to the beads. But then at the last second, she jumped off into the grass. Her mom started yelling at her, and then she veered back onto the sidewalk. Unfortunately, she had already passed the beads. I started to get worried that no one might step on them. But then the mom, who was hot on her daughter's trail, took a giant step right onto them and flew way up into the air. She landed with a hard thud. Jasmine and I shared a quick high four. She started yelling tons of interesting words that I'd never heard before, and everyone came rushing to her aid. The husband slowly helped her to her feet, asking what happened. Then he bent down to examine the ground, and he picked up the clear bead. Angrily he showed it to the realtor asking her if this was some sort of cruel prank.

"No," she said, shaking her head, "I have no clue where those came from, but I can assure you it wasn't me."

"Alright whatever," he said, "Let's just get into the house so we can sign the final paperwork." The mom slowly got up clutching her hip, and the group of people started moving again. But this time with the son at the head of the pack. He was just starting to flip a page of his book when his foot got caught on the line we had strung. He tumbled straight forward, with his head still down. He landed straight on his face and let out a huge scream. Yet again, the father came rushing over. He bent down to check on his son when he noticed the string. This time he let out a thunderous roar, as he pulled it straight off the bush and mailbox. Once again, he showed it to the realtor, demanding to know what was going on. Of course, she didn't know why that was there, so she shook her head just as confused as he was.

"No more funny business," he said, as he lifted his son off the ground and started marching straight for the door. At that point, Jasmine gave some sort of signal to the pigeons and they took flight.

The flock of them circled around the back of the house in the air and flew straight overhead of the people. What they did next even shocked me. The whole lot of them dropped their smelly white poop right onto the dad's head. He was doused from head to toe in pigeon poop. At this point, that was just about all he could handle. He let out a rageful scream so loud I thought it would shatter the windows.

He tried to flick off as much of it as possible, but most of it was soaked into his clothes. He was angry now. By this time he was only 10 feet or so away from the porch and was getting closer very quickly. Jasmine and I didn't have any other lines of defense set up. And when I looked over to the side of the house, I could still see mice evacuating. I knew I had to stop him somehow. So just as he stepped onto the porch, I did the only reasonable thing I could think of.

I jumped right out from behind the railing and charged at him. Ok, I wouldn't say charged at him, but I ran as fast as I could straight at his leg. This sent him over the edge. He started stomping and kicking as hard as he could at me. I was doing all I could to avoid him when he caught me with his kick and sent me flying straight over the edge of the porch.

I feel upwards of 4 feet straight onto the ground. I don't even remember landing, because it knocked me straight out. All I can remember was seeing Jasmine reaching for me and yelling

"Noooo." There was also one other thing I remember seeing before I blacked out... When the dad kicked me, he actually ended up stepping right on the slipperiest part of the porch. His feet went right up from under him, and he slipped right over the opposite edge of the porch.

Hope Is Restored

I wouldn't wake up for two whole days after that. When I did wake up, I was greeted by plenty of concerned mice; Max, Jasmine, and my mother all included. It sounded like the three of them didn't leave my side once during those two days. My mom started shooing everyone away from me saying I needed my rest and some peace and quiet. I took in the room around me while all that was happening. It looked like we were inside the big hollowed-out tree, and I seemed to be laying in a comfortable enough bed on the far left side of the room. The room was filled to the brim with everyone from the Oasis. There were also dozens of cards lining the wall next to me wishing for my speedy recovery.

    Once most everyone had cleared off Jasmine and Max were able to give me an update of everything that had happened the last two days. Apparently, after the dad fell off the porch, he and the rest of his family hobbled off towards their car yelling the deal was off. The realtor had chased after them apologizing saying she didn't know what was going on, but it was final they weren't buying the house after all.

    Max told me that Jasmine, with the help of some remaining mice, had carried me all the way to this tree. She had some help from some of the remaining evacuating mice. She had gotten me to my mother who immediately determined I had a broken arm, and got me all fixed up. My mom had also said I had a concussion and needed to stay in bed for many days following.

    He also told me that earlier today the agents who had been sent out to retrieve the family from our previous mission had returned safely with the family. Apparently, the family was settling in nicely. That was good news.

Then he went on to tell me even better news. When Jasmine and I were stalling the people, we did such a great job that we scared them and every possible buyer away. The dad had now stood outside the house for the last two days telling anyone that would listen what a terrible house it was. There's been no one else visiting the house, and by the looks of it, it is going to stay empty.

"Wait," I said, "does this mean that we 'll be able to live there again?" I asked hopefully.

"Ya," Jasmine said. "The mayor had a town meeting last night saying that Samy Soon's will be keeping surveillance on the house. If nothing is happening there through next week, he thinks it'll be safe to go back. He also informed everyone that this good fortune would not have happened without the two of us. He even added Max for his supporting role. But the point is, we're celebrities around here. Everywhere I turn mice are trying to give me their thanks, and random gifts. You just wait till you're up and walking, you'll never have a free second to yourself." I was so happy to hear this. I hadn't even thought about saving the Oasis, but it looked like we did.

    The next week dragged on super slowly. I was so excited to get back home, I could barely wait. To help the time go by faster, Jasmine, Max, and I would sneak away when my mother wasn't looking and go down to the stream. We'd spend countless hours down there, and when Max was off in the stream, Jasmine and I would hold hands and talk about basically everything. I think Max wandered away for so long because he saw how happy I was for the first time in a long time.

    I was able to meet the family who was rescued by those agents. I told them all about our efforts to save them, and how sorry I was. But the mother wouldn't hear of it. She was so grateful for our effort, and she even told us all about the time they had spent with the exterminator. Apparently, he was planning on selling them to a pet store, but the agents arrived just in the nick of time.

    Finally, the week was up. Since there was no activity at the Oasis, the mayor gave the go-ahead to start moving back in. Mice were allowed to travel in pairs of 10 back to the Oasis, so as not to draw a lot of attention to us. After quite a long day, everyone was back home inside the Oasis. It took days to get the place back up and running, but it was so worth it. Being back in our home was an amazing feeling because most of us thought we'd never be back here.

Safe At Last

Over the next couple of weeks, we made some big changes around the Oasis. The first one was to thank both the Crawlers from the sewer and the West Park pigeon flock for their roles in saving the Oasis. We sent out invitations to both of the groups to come live with us here in the Oasis. Both of them showed up only hours after the invitations were sent gratefully accepting them. Even the Mayor and his brother made up for their past problems.

Everyone young and old worked countless hours to dig more tunnels in the house for the rats. We gave the untouched attic to the pigeons so they could fly in and out as they pleased. All three groups were able to live peacefully together to create an even better Oasis. Even Matilda was finally able to get along with us. I don't know what changed, but one day she came into the house and instead of attacking us, she just slept. In fact, every day after that, when she came into the house she slept for hours and never once bothered us.

Now let's jump forward to the years following those crazy couple weeks that changed life at the Oasis as we knew it. To start, Jasmine and I ended up getting married. We have two kids of our own, their names are Sally and James. They annoy the crap out of me, but I still love them. We also built our own house in the tunnels. We still work at Samy Soon's, but after Ms. Cricket retired, I took over the head position. The two of us still go out on missions together and I'm living my best life.

Max ended up marrying Trina, and they live right across the tunnel from us. They didn't end up having kids, because they like to party a lot throughout the week. The four of us make sure to get together at least once a week for game nights and delicious dinners. Max and I also go on walks around the house every morning.

My mother is still doing what she loves, teaching young mice. My sister Lily still lives with her in our childhood home. Lily also started teaching not too long ago, and by golly, she's good at it. All my brothers moved out and started families of their own, so I don't see them very often.

The Oasis has grown into an amazing community of all sorts of creatures. Our doors are always open to anyone in need. We've become well known around Main with animals, and have dedicated the whole basement of the house to animals of all kinds who are avoiding exterminators. I guess you could say everything worked out in the end for us rodents. It looks like humans don't win every time.

Made in the USA
Middletown, DE
13 August 2023

36482399R00046